Ashland, Ohio 44805

POCAHONTAS

STORYBOOK

Pocahontas was an Indian princess who lived many years ago along a broad river which flowed to the sea.

It was a land where trees grew near the water, and animals of many kinds came to the river to drink.

The only people living there were Indians, whose homes were cozy shelters made of brush and hide which they called wigwams.

Pocahontas lived in the largest of these wigwams, for she was the daughter of the mighty chief Powhatan, and she was his favorite child.

She wore a dress of deerskin trimmed in beads made from shells, and her long dark hair was braided and tied with twisted vines. Her mother had tucked in two feathers at the top to keep track of Pocahontas as she dashed about the camp in play. She spent many happy hours learning about the forest and the river.

One day strange new people from a faraway land arrived in big boats which were blown by the wind and needed no paddles.

They had come from a country called England on the other side of the ocean, and had many things like guns and steel axes, which were new to Pocahontas and her people.

The Indians watched with caution as these new people began to build a settlement with strange looking houses.

Pocahontas saw the leader of the new people come to her village to trade one day. His name was Captain John Smith, and he was a soldier who wore bright steel armor and carried a gun which made a loud noise.

She had noticed him many times before in the forest, and thought that he was a good brave man.

But this day, the warriors of her father's tribe were angry about things the new people had done.

The warriors worried because the new people were taking more and more land their tribe needed for hunting and planting.

They captured Captain Smith and held a meeting to decide his fate. Pocahontas sat quietly at the edge of the group around the council fire, waiting to hear someone tell of the good things the visitors had brought them, but they decided his fate would be death.

When Pocahontas heard this she was very sad and, although she was just a young girl, she ran to John Smith's side and pleaded with her father to spare the Captain's life.

Powhatan saw how much this meant to his favorite daughter, and ordered his warriors to cause no harm to Captain Smith. He decided that if Pocahontas was able to see the good in the new settlers, then maybe they *could* live together in peace.

Pocahontas became good friends with John Smith and the other people of the new village. Captain Smith taught her English customs and gave her gifts of beads and clothes in gratitude for her kindness and brave actions.

He learned that many of the Indian ways were best for those who lived in this new land, and Pocahontas found that there was much she could learn from his people as well.

Because they did not know how to survive in the blistery forest, the new settlers had trouble finding enough to eat the first winter in their new settlement.

Pocahontas brought them food and showed them where to find fish in the streams, and nuts and berries in the forests.

The Indian princess became a heroine to everyone in the new colony. They taught this brave girl how to read and write their language, and Pocahontas showed them many Indian customs and rituals to help them understand each other better.

Eventually, Pocahontas decided to stay in Jamestown with Captain John Smith and the new settlers. There she met and married John Rolfe, who loved her and this beautiful new land.

They built a cabin, and Pocahontas was given the English name of Rebecca. Her husband soon decided he wanted people in his homeland to meet his Indian princess, and Pocahontas agreed to go. Even though she would be sad to leave her own homeland, she looked forward to the new experiences traveling to England would bring.

Pocahontas and her family voyaged back to England on one of the huge ships with sails that let it move by the power of the wind. John Rolfe presented her to the King and his court, where Captain John Smith had already spoke of her kindness and bravery, and she charmed everyone.

Pocahontas stayed in England, where her husband had an important position, and she was called "The Lady Rebecca." Her children returned to America when they were grown, and helped build this new country.